Gg Hh Ii Jj Kk Ll Mm

Uu Vv Ww Xx Yy Zz

Dear Parent,

The My First Steps to Reading® *series is based on a teaching activity that helps children learn to recognize letters and their sounds. The use of predictable language patterns and repetition of familiar words will also help your child build a basic sight vocabulary. Your child will enjoy watching the characters in the books place imaginative objects in "letter boxes." You and your child can even create and fill your own letter box, using stuffed animals, cut-out pictures, or other objects beginning with the same letter. The things you can do together are limited only by your imagination. Learning letters will be fun—the first important step on the road to reading.*

The Editors

All Rights Reserved. Published by Scholastic Inc., 90 Old Sherman Turnpike, Danbury, Connecticut 06810,
by arrangement with The Child's World, Inc.
Scholastic offers a varied selection of children's book racks and tote bags. For details about ordering, please write to:
Scholastic At Home, 90 Old Sherman Turnpike, Danbury, CT 06810, Attention: Premium Department

Originally published as *My "r" Sound Box* by The Child's World, Inc.

My First Steps to Reading is a registered trademark of Grolier Publishing Co. Inc.
SCHOLASTIC and associated logos are trademarks and/or registered trademarks of Scholastic Inc.

Printed in the U.S.A.

My "r" Book

written by Jane Belk Moncure

illustrated by Colin King

Little  had a box.

"I will find things that begin with my 'r' sound," he said. "I will put them into my sound box."

Little  found rabbits and radishes.

Did he put the rabbits and radishes into his box? He did.

Little  found a rooster.

Did he put the rooster into the box with the rabbits and radishes? He did.

Then he found a raccoon.

The raccoon ran!

Little ran after the raccoon . . .

and put him into the  box.

Then he saw a rat.

The rat ran.

Little  ran after the rat

and put him into the box.

Then he ran down the road.

Soon Little  met a reindeer.

The reindeer was too big for the box. So Little found a boat he could row.

In it, he put the reindeer and the box with the rat, the raccoon, the rooster, and the rabbits.

There were no radishes left.
The rabbits had eaten the radishes.

Little

rowed down the river.

But it rained.

Little put on his raincoat.

He rowed right into a . . .

rhinoceros.

The rhinoceros was too big

for the boat.

So Little r found a raft.

He put all the animals onto the raft.
He put the box onto the raft, too.

But the raft ran into a rock.

The reindeer, the rat, and the rooster
fell off the raft.

Little r found

a rope . . .

and rescued them!

"Now we will rest!" he said.

The rhinoceros, the rabbits, the raccoon, the reindeer, the rat, and the rooster rested . . .

under a rainbow.

Little rested, too.

Then the rabbits said, "Let's run a race."

They ran up the road to . . .

a bush full of 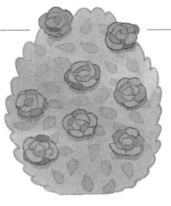 roses.

Little  picked roses for his box.

"Let's play ring-around-the-rosy," he said. And they did.

raft

rainbow

reindeer

rhinoceros

roses

rabbits

rooster

rat

raccoon

27

Can you read these words with Little 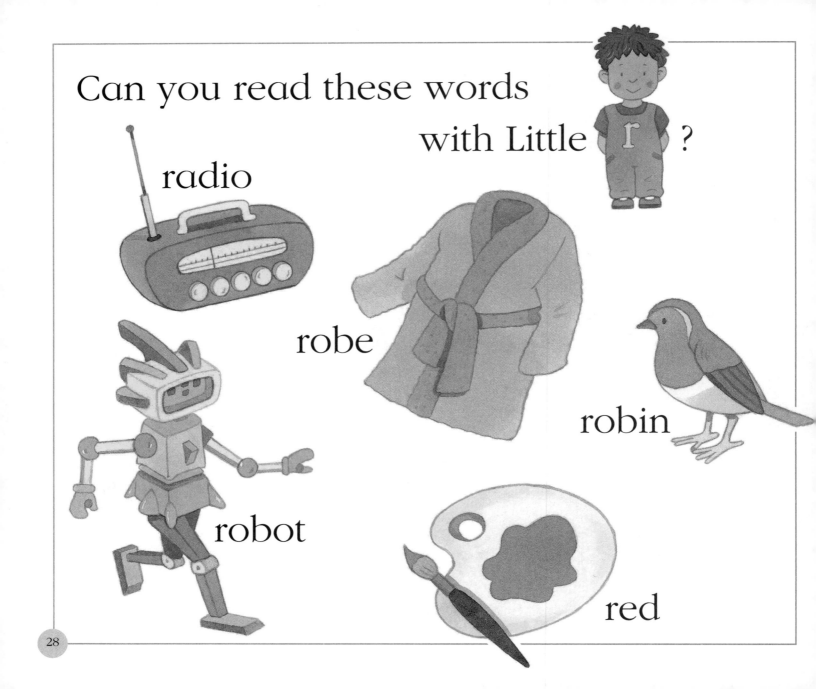 ?

radio

robe

robin

robot

red

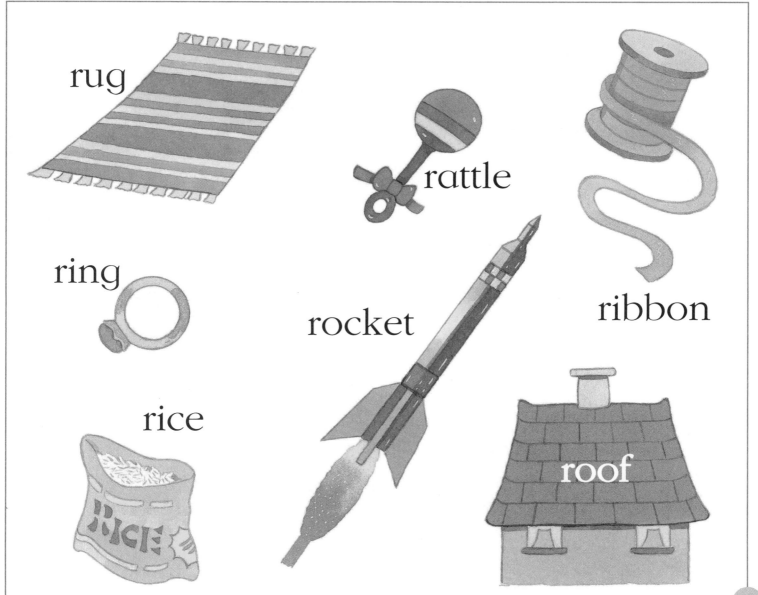

rug

rattle

ribbon

ring

rocket

rice

roof

Aa Bb Cc Dd Ee Ff

Nn Oo Pp Qq Rr Ss Tt

My First Steps to READING®